The Bill Martin Jr BIG BOOK of POETRY

The Bill Martin Jr BIG BOOK of POETRY

edited by

Bill Martin Jr

with Michael Sampson

foreword by Eric Carle

afterword by Steven Kellogg

Simon & Schuster Books for Young Readers
New York London Toronto Sydney

ACKNOWLEDGMENTS

Grateful acknowledgment is made for permission to reprint the copyrighted material listed below:

All Things Press for "Papa Says" from BOX OF PEPPERMINTS by Libby Stopple. Copyright 1975 by All Things Press. Reproduced with permission of All Things Press via Copyright Clearance Center.

Curtis Brown, Ltd. for "This Tooth." Copyright 1970 by Lee Bennett Hopkins. First appeared in ME!, published by Seabury Press. "Under the Microscope." Copyright 1999 by Lee Bennett Hopkins. First appeared in SPECTACULAR SCIENCE, published by Simon & Schuster, Inc. "Subways Are People." Copyright 1971 by Lee Bennett Hopkins. First appeared in FACES AND PLACES AND POEMS FOR YOU, published by Scholastic, Inc. "A Social Mixer." Copyright 1975 by X. J. Kennedy. First appeared in ONE WINTER NIGHT IN AUGUST AND OTHER NONSENSE JINGLES, published by Atheneum. "My Little Sister." Copyright 1971 by William Wise. First appeared in ALL ON A SUMMER DAY, published by Pantheon. Reprinted by permission of Curtis Brown, Ltd.

The Estate of Bill Martin Jr for "Let There Be Pizza on Earth" by Bill Martin Jr and David Canzoneri. "City Song," "Old Mother Hubbard," and "Once Upon a Time" by Bill Martin Jr and Michael Sampson. "Ten Little Caterpillars" by Bill Martin Jr. Used by permission of the Estate of Bill Martin Jr.

Lillian M. Fisher for "Child of the Sun." Used by permission of the author who controls all rights.

Martin Gardner for "Speak Clearly."

Harcourt, Inc. for "The Folk Who Live in Backward Town" and "Foxes" from THE LLAMA WHO HAD NO PAJAMA: 100 FAVORITE POEMS. Copyright 1998 by Mary Ann Hoberman. "To Look at Any Thing" from THE LIVING SEED. Copyright 1961 by John Moffitt and renewed 1989 by Henry Moffitt. Reprinted by permission of Harcourt, Inc.

Harold Ober Associates, Inc. for "A Kitten" by Eleanor Farjeon. Copyright 1933, renewed 1961 by Eleanor Farjeon. Reprinted by permission of Harold Ober Associates Incorporated.

HarperCollins Publishers for "Mummy Slept Late and Daddy Fixed Breakfast" by John Ciardi. Copyright © 1962 by John Ciardi. Used by permission of HarperCollins Publishers. "Knoxville, Tennessee" from BLACK FEELING, BLACK TALK, BLACK JUDGMENT by Nikki Giovanni. Copyright 1968, 1970 by Nikki Giovanni. "Kitty Caught a Caterpillar." Text © 1986 by Jack Prelutsky. Used by permission of HarperCollins Publishers. "I Am Running in a Circle" and "I've Got an Itch" from THE NEW KID ON THE BLOCK by Jack Prelutsky. Copyright 1984 by Jack Prelutsky. Reprinted by permission of HarperCollins Publishers. "Herbert Glerbett" by Jack Prelutsky. Text copyright © 1978 by Jack Prelutsky. Used by permission of HarperCollins Publishers. "The Park." Copyright © 1927 by James S. Tippett. Used by permission of HarperCollins Publishers. "I Keep Three Wishes Ready" by Annette Wynne. Copyright © 1932 by Annette Wynne.

Harvard Management Company, Inc. for "Something Told the Wild Geese" from BRANCHES GREEN by Rachel Field, published by the Macmillan Company in 1934, and "The Little Rose Tree" from THE POINTED PEOPLE by Rachel Field, published by the Macmillan Company in 1930. Reprinted by permission of the Trustees of the Pederson Trust.

Harvard University Press for "A bird came down the walk" from THE POEMS OF EMILY DICKINSON, Thomas H. Johnson, ed., Cambridge, Mass.: The Belknap Press of Harvard University Press. Copyright 1951, 1955, 1979, 1983 by the President and Fellows of Harvard College. Reprinted by permission of the publishers and the Trustees of Amherst College.

Elizabeth Hauser for "Spring Rain" and "My Dog" from AROUND AND ABOUT by Marchette Chute, published 1957 by E.P. Dutton. Copyright renewed by Marchette Chute, 1985. "Sleeping Outdoors" from RHYMES ABOUT US by Marchette Chute, published 1974 by E.P. Dutton. Reprinted by permission of Elizabeth Hauser.

Henry Holt & Co., LLC for "Stopping by Woods on a Snowy Evening" from THE POETRY OF ROBERT FROST edited by Edward Connery Lathem. Copyright 1923, 1969 by Henry Holt and Company. Copyright 1951 by Robert Frost. Reprinted by permission of Henry Holt and Company, LLC.

Lee & Low Books, Inc. for "in daddy's arms," a poem from the collection IN DADDY'S ARMS I AM TALL. Copyright 1997 by Folami Abiade. "Promises," a poem from the collection IN DADDY'S ARMS I AM TALL. Copyright 1997 by David A. Anderson. Permission arranged with Lee & Low Books, Inc., New York, NY 10016.

Lescher & Lescher, Ltd. for "Some Things Don't Make Any Sense at All," and "If I Were in Charge of the World" by Judith Viorst, from IF I WERE IN CHARGE OF THE WORLD AND OTHER WORRIES. Published by Atheneum Books for Young Readers, an imprint of Simon & Schuster Children's Publishing Division. Copyright 1981 by Judith Viorst. Reprinted by permission of Simon & Schuster and Lescher & Lescher, Ltd. All rights reserved.

The Literary Estate of May Swenson for "Painting the Gate" by May Swenson. Used with permission of the Literary Estate of May Swenson.

Little, Brown and Company for "Vacation" from FATHERS, MOTHERS, SISTERS, BROTHERS by Mary Ann Hoberman. Copyright 1991 by Mary Ann Hoberman (Text). Copyright 1991 by Marylin Hafner (Illustrations). By permission of Little, Brown and Co., Inc.

Gina Maccoby Literary Agency for "The Folk Who Live in Backward Town" by Mary Ann Hoberman. Copyright 1959, renewed 1987 by Mary Ann Hoberman. Reprinted by permission of the Gina Maccoby Literary Agency.

Beverly McLoughland for "SOS," which first appeared in *Instructor's Magazine*, February 1988. Author controls all rights.

Ann Whitford Paul for "Word Builder."

Pearson Education, Inc. for "Oodles of Noodles" and "Tombstone" from OODLES OF NOODLES. Copyright 1964 Lucia and James Hymes Jr. "Beans, Beans, Beans" from HOORAY FOR CHOCOLATE. Copyright 1960 Lucia and James L. Hymes Jr. Reproduced by permission of Pearson Education, Inc. All rights reserved.

Penguin Group (USA) Inc. for "Bursting" and "Kick a Little Stone" from ALL TOGETHER by Dorothy Aldis. Copyright 1925–1928, 1934, 1939, 1952, renewed 1953. © 1954–56, 1962 by Dorothy Aldis, © 1967 by Roy E. Porter, renewed. Used by permission of G.P. Putnam's Sons, A Division of Penguin Young Readers Group, A Member of Penguin Group (USA) Inc., 345 Hudson Street, New York, NY 10014. "Taking Turns," from SMALL WONDERS by Norma Farber. Copyright © 1964, 1968, 1975, 1976, 1978, 1979 by Norma Farber. Used by permission of Coward-McCann, A Division of Penguin Young Readers Group, A Member of Penguin Group (USA) Inc., 345 Hudson Street, New York, NY 10014. "The Woodpecker," from UNDER THE TREE by Elizabeth Maddox Roberts. Copyright 1922 by B.W. Huebsch, Inc., renewed 1950 by Ivor S. Roberts. Copyright 1930 by Viking Penguin, renewed © 1958 by Ivor S. Roberts & Viking Penguin. Used by permission of Viking Penguin, A Division of Penguin Young Readers Group, A Member of Penguin Group (USA) Inc., 345 Hudson Street, New York, NY 10014. All rights reserved.

Louis Phillips for "On Eating Porridge Made of Peas," which originally appeared in THE DAY EVERYBODY WAS IN A BAD MOOD, Prologue Press (Copyright 1975). Reprinted by permission of the author.

Random House, Inc. for "Eyes in the Night" and "So Many Nights" from THE GOLDEN SLEEPY BOOK by Margaret Wise Brown and Garth Williams, illustrator. Copyright 1948, renewed 1976 by Random House, Inc. Used by permission of Golden Books, an imprint of Random House Children's Books, a division of Random House, Inc. "New Year's Day" from A LITTLE BOOK OF DAYS by Rachel Field. Copyright 1927 by Doubleday, a division of Random House, Inc. Used by permission of Doubleday, a division of Random House, Inc. "Grandpa's Stories," "Dreamer," and "April Rain Song" from THE COLLECTED POEMS OF LANGSTON HUGHES by Langston Hughes, edited by Arnold Rampersad with David Roessel, Associate Editor. Copyright 1994 by the Estate of Langston Hughes. Used by permission of Alfred A. Knopf, a division of Random House, Inc., and reprinted by permission of Harold Ober Associates Incorporated. "Skyscraper" and "Dickery Dean" from DINOSAUR DINNER (WITH A SLICE OF ALLIGATOR PIE) by Dennis Lee. Copyright Compilation © 1997 by Alfred A. Knopf, Inc. Text © 1974, 1977, 1983, 1991 by Dennis Lee. Illustrations © 1997 by Debbie Tilley. Used by permission of Alfred A. Knopf, an imprint of Random House Children's Books, a division of Random House, Inc.

Marian Reiner for "Climbing," "Snail's Pace," and "Open House" from IN THE WOODS, IN THE MEADOW, IN THE SKY by Aileen Fisher. Copyright © 1965 by Aileen Fisher. "Caterpillars" from CRICKET IN A THICKET by Aileen Fisher. Copyright © 1963 by Aileen Fisher. "Baby Chick" and "Wise" from RUNNY DAYS, SUNNY DAYS by Aileen Fisher. Copyright © 1958 Aileen Fisher. "The First Day of School" from OUT IN THE DARK AND DAYLIGHT by Aileen Fisher. Copyright © 1946 by Aileen Fisher. "O Sliver of Liver" from O SLIVER OF LIVER AND OTHER POEMS by Myra Cohn Livingston. Copyright © 1979 Myra Cohn Livingston. "My Star" from THE MOON AND A STAR AND OTHER POEMS by Myra Cohn Livingston. Copyright © 1965 Myra Cohn Livingston. "The Dark" from WORLDS I KNOW AND OTHER POEMS by Myra Cohn Livingston. Copyright © 1985 Myra Cohn Livingston. "Metaphor" from A SKY FULL OF POEMS by Eve Merriam. Copyright © 1964, 1970, 1973, 1986 by Eve Merriam. "Take a Number" from TAKE A NUMBER by Mary O'Neill. Copyright © 1968 Mary O'Neill, renewed 1996 by Erin Baroni and Abigail Hagler. "Eat-It-All Elaine" from DON'T EVER CROSS A CROCODILE by Kaye Starbird. Copyright © 1963 by Kaye Starbird. Used by permission of Marian Reiner.

S©ott Treimel NY for "Tiptoe" from IN THE MIDDLE OF THE TREES by Karla Kuskin. Copyright © 1959, renewed 1986 by Karla Kuskin. Reprinted by permission of S©ott Treimel NY.

Simon & Schuster, Inc. for "In the Woods," "Green Grass & Dandelions," "Postman's Song," and "Christmas Song" from GIVE YOURSELF TO THE RAIN by Margaret Wise Brown. Text copyright © 2002 Roberta Brown Rauch. Reprinted with the permission of Margaret K. McElderry Books, an imprint of Simon & Schuster Children's Publishing Division. "Pick Me, Please" from DON'T READ THIS BOOK, WHATEVER YOU DO! by Kalli Dakos. Text copyright © 1993 Kalli Dakos. "I Brought a Worm" and "Poor Substitute" from IF YOU'RE NOT HERE, PLEASE RAISE YOUR HAND by Kalli Dakos. Text copyright © 1990 Kalli Dakos. Reprinted with the permission of Simon & Schuster Books for Young Readers, an imprint of Simon & Schuster Children's Publishing Division. "Manhattan Lullaby" from POEMS by Rachel Field. Copyright 1946 Macmillan Publishing Company; copyright renewed 1964 Arthur S. Pederson. "Something Told the Wild Geese" from POEMS by Rachel Field. Copyright 1934 Macmillan Publishing Company; copyright renewed © 1962 Arthur S. Pederson. Reprinted with the permission of Simon & Schuster Books for Young Readers, an imprint of Simon & Schuster Children's Publishing Division. "The Dark" from WORLDS I KNOW AND OTHER POEMS by Myra Cohn Livingston. Text copyright © 1985 Myra Cohn Livingston. Reprinted with the permission of Margaret K. McElderry Books, an imprint of Simon & Schuster Children's Publishing Division.

The Society of Authors for "Mice" by Rose Fyleman. Used by permission of the Society of Authors as the Literary Representative of the Estate of Rose Fyleman.

Colin West for "Norman Norton's Nostrils." Reprinted with permission of the author.

Westwood Creative Artists Ltd. for "Dickery Dean" by Dennis Lee, from JELLY BELLY (Macmillan of Canada, 1983). Copyright © 1983 Dennis Lee. "The Muddy Puddle" by Dennis Lee, from GARBAGE DELIGHT (Macmillan of Canada, 1977). Copyright © 1977 Dennis Lee. "Skyscraper" by Dennis Lee, from ALLIGATOR PIE (Macmillan of Canada, 1974; Key Porter Books, 2001). Copyright © 1974 Dennis Lee. With permission of the author.

SIMON & SCHUSTER BOOKS FOR YOUNG READERS · An imprint of Simon & Schuster Children's Publishing Division · 1230 Avenue of the Americas, New York, New York 10020 · Compilation copyright © 2008 by Michael Sampson · Illustrations copyright © 2008 by Simon & Schuster, Inc. · Includes art by Aliki (pages 43, 48, 49, 84, 85, 97, 103, 106–7, 110, 127, 134); Derek Anderson (pages 34, 46, 63, 87, 111, 140–41, 150, 166, 167); Ashley Bryan (pages 14–15, 36–37, 122–23, 164–65); Henry Cole (pages 64, 65, 74, 102, 115, 126, 139, 152–53, 168); Lois Ehlert (pages 5, 16, 25, 90–94); David Gordon (pages 41, 80–81, 104, 108, 117, 119, 125, 163); Steven Kellogg (pages 11, 72, 100–101, 112, 133, 147, 154–55, 161, 170–71); Laura Logan (pages 35, 44, 47, 53, 59, 70, 75, 78, 86, 95, 113, 116, 128, 135, 136, 160); Paul Meisel (pages 20, 28–29, 54, 68–69, 77, 88–89, 105, 118, 132, 146, 151, 162); Robert Quackenbush (pages 17, 21, 32, 38, 52, 55, 58, 76, 129, 148, 149, 158–59); Chris Raschka (pages 18–19, 22, 30, 45, 56, 57, 79, 109, 114, 137, 144–45, 169); Nancy Tafuri (pages 24, 31, 33, 39, 61, 62, 73); Dan Yaccarino (pages 23, 40, 42, 60, 71, 96, 124, 138). · All rights reserved, including the right of reproduction in whole or in part in any form. · SIMON & SCHUSTER BOOKS FOR YOUNG READERS is a trademark of Simon & Schuster, Inc. · Book design by Edward Miller and Lucy Ruth Cummins · The text for this book is set in New Century Schoolbook. · The illustrations for this book are rendered in a variety of media. · Manufactured in China · 10 9 8 7 6 5 4 3 2 1 · CIP data for this book is available from the Library of Congress. · ISBN-13: 978-1-4169-3971-9 · ISBN-10: 1-4169-3971-7

first edition

Dedicated
to the
memory of

BILL B M MARTIN JR

Contents

Foreword

Bill Martin Jr: Editor, Writer, Educator, Poet, and National Treasure

In 1992 Bill and I were on a signing tour together for *Polar Bear, Polar Bear, What Do You Hear?,* the second book on which we had collaborated. Twenty-five years earlier I had illustrated his text for *Brown Bear, Brown Bear, What Do You See?* One morning Bill came to join me in the breakfast room of the elegant hotel in which we were staying. He told me that he had been up most of the night working on a story. Would I be interested in hearing what he had written? Holding up a sheet of paper he read, "Dum-da-da, dum-da-da, dum," and then asked if I thought that "Da-da-dum, da-dum, da-dum" would be better.

"Bill," I asked, "what are you talking about? What kind of a story is that?"

"Oh, first I always establish the rhythm."

Then, while he waited for his cereal with berries and I for my French toast with maple syrup, Bill told me the most astonishing fact: All through elementary school and part of high school he was unable to read. He was somehow able to fake it until his late teens, when an understanding teacher confronted him and taught him to read through rhythm. (I assume with *Da-da-dum*'s!) Not many years later Bill earned a doctorate in education.

"Were you dyslexic?" I asked.

"No. It was fear," he replied.

Discovering the rhythms underlying the written words was an exhilarating experience for the shy boy. It had brought him comfort and eventually joy in reading.

Before we are born, we are surrounded and supported by the steady heartbeat of our mother. I suspect that throughout our lives we attempt to recapture the distant rhythm of that reassuring heartbeat. That is where Bill's genius has its roots. And that, in a way, is what art is about. The art of Rembrandt, Shakespeare, Mozart. All art touches and releases the spring that lies deep within us. In his selection of poems for his *Big Book of Poetry*, Bill Martin Jr's sure instinct is again evident.

—Eric Carle

The Pasture

I'm going out to clean the pasture spring;
I'll only stop to rake the leaves away
(And wait to watch the clear water, I may):
I shan't be gone long—You come too.

I'm going out to fetch the little calf
That's standing by the mother. It's too young,
It totters when she licks it with her tongue.
I shan't be gone long—You come too.

Robert Frost

Illustration by Steven Kellogg

Animals

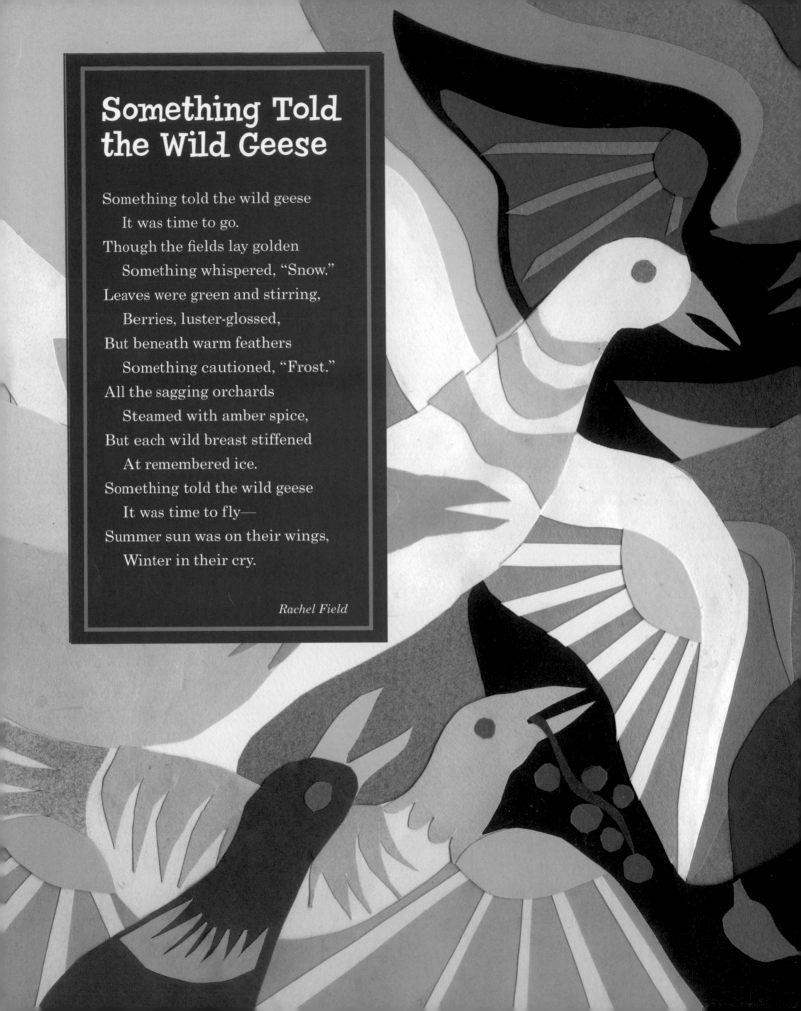

Something Told the Wild Geese

Something told the wild geese
   It was time to go.
Though the fields lay golden
   Something whispered, "Snow."
Leaves were green and stirring,
   Berries, luster-glossed,
But beneath warm feathers
   Something cautioned, "Frost."
All the sagging orchards
   Steamed with amber spice,
But each wild breast stiffened
   At remembered ice.
Something told the wild geese
   It was time to fly—
Summer sun was on their wings,
   Winter in their cry.

Rachel Field

Illustration by Ashley Bryan

Mice

I think mice
Are rather nice.

Their tails are long,
Their faces small,
They haven't any
Chins at all.
Their ears are pink,
Their teeth are white,
They run about
The house at night.
They nibble things
They shouldn't touch
And no one seems
To like them much.

But *I* think mice
Are nice.

Rose Fyleman

Illustration by Lois Ehlert

Caterpillars

What do caterpillars do?
Nothing much but chew and chew.

What do caterpillars know?
Nothing much but how to grow.

They just eat what by and by
Will make them be a butterfly,

But that is more that I can do
However much I chew and chew.

Aileen L. Fisher

Illustration by Robert Quackenbush

The Wolf

When the pale moon hides and the wild wind wails,
And over the tree-tops the nighthawk sails,
The gray wolf sits on the world's far rim,
And howls: and it seems to comfort him.

The wolf is a lonely soul, you see,
No beast in the wood, nor bird in the tree,
But shuns his path; in the windy gloom
They give him plenty, and plenty of room.

So he sits with his long, lean face to the sky
Watching the ragged clouds go by.
There in the night, alone, apart,
Singing the song of his lone, wild heart.

Far away, on the world's dark rim
He howls, and it seems to comfort him.

Georgia Roberts Durston

Illustration by Chris Raschka

A Bird Came Down the Walk

A bird came down the walk:
He did not know I saw;

He bit an angle-worm in halves
And ate the fellow, raw.

And then he drank a dew
From a convenient grass,

And then hopped sidewise to the wall
To let a beetle pass.

Emily Dickinson

Illustration by Paul Meisel

20

Baby Chick

Peck, peck, peck
on the warm brown egg.
Out comes a neck!
Out comes a leg!

How does a chick,
who's not been about,
discover the trick
of how to get out?

Aileen L. Fisher

Illustration by Robert Quackenbush

A Kitten

He's nothing much but fur
And two round eyes of blue,
He has a giant purr
And a midget mew.

He darts and pats the air,
He starts and cocks his ear,
When there is nothing there
For him to see and hear.

He runs around in rings,
But why we cannot tell;
With sideways leaps he springs
At things invisible—

Then half-way through a leap
His startled eyeballs close,
And he drops off to sleep
With one paw on his nose.

Eleanor Farjeon

Illustration by Chris Raschka

Crocodile

If you should meet a crocodile
Don't take a stick and poke him;
Ignore the welcome in his smile,
Be careful not to stroke him.
For as he sleeps upon the Nile,
He thinner gets and thinner;
Whenever you meet a crocodile
He's looking for his dinner.

Anonymous

Illustration by Dan Yaccarino

Foxes

A litter of little black foxes. And later
A litter of little gray foxes. And later
A litter of little white foxes.
The white ones are lighter than gray. Not a lot.
The gray ones are lighter than black. Just a little.
The litters are lighter in moonlight. They glitter.
They gleam in the moonlight. They glow and they glisten.
Out on the snow see the silver fox sparkle.

Mary Ann Hoberman

Illustration by Nancy Tafuri

The Woodpecker

The woodpecker pecked out a little round hole
And made him a house in the telephone pole.

One day when I watched he poked out his head,
And he had on a hood and a collar of red.

When the streams of rain pour out of the sky,
And the sparkles of lightning go flashing by,

And the big, big wheels of thunder roll,
He can snuggle back in the telephone pole.

Elizabeth Maddox Roberts

Illustration by Lois Ehlert

World of Nature

Weather

Whether the weather be fine,
Or whether the weather be not,
Whether the weather be cold,
Or whether the weather be hot,
We'll weather the weather
Whatever the weather,
Whether we like it or not!

Anonymous

Illustration by Paul Meisel

Clouds

White sheep, white sheep
On a blue hill,
When the wind stops
You all stand still.
When the wind blows
You walk away slow.
White sheep, white sheep
Where do you go?

Christina G. Rossetti

Illustration by Chris Raschka

Who Has Seen the Wind?

Who has seen the wind?
Neither I nor you;
But when the leaves hang trembling
The wind is passing through.

Who has seen the wind?
Neither you nor I;
But when the trees bow down their heads
The wind is passing by.

Christina G. Rossetti

Illustration by Nancy Tafuri

The Muddy Puddle

I am sitting
In the middle
Of a rather Muddy
Puddle,
With my bottom
Full of bubbles
And my rubbers
Full of Mud,
While my jacket
And my sweater
Go on slowly
Getting wetter
As I very
Slowly settle
To the Bottom
Of the Mud.
And I find that
What a person
With a puddle
Round his middle
Thinks of mostly
In the muddle
Is the Muddi-
Ness of Mud.

Dennis Lee

Illustration by Robert Quackenbush

Fog

The fog comes
on little cat feet.

It sits looking
over harbor and city
on silent haunches
and then moves on.

Carl Sandburg

Illustration by Nancy Tafuri

Spring Rain

The storm came up so very quick
    It couldn't have been quicker.
I should have brought my hat along,
    I should have brought my slicker.

My hair is wet, my feet are wet,
    I couldn't be much wetter.
I fell into a river once
    But this is even better.

Marchette Chute

Illustration by Derek Anderson

The Rainbow

Boats sail on the rivers,
    And ships sail on the seas;
But clouds that sail across the sky
    Are prettier far than these.

There are bridges on the rivers,
    As pretty as you please;
But the bow that bridges heaven,
    And overtops the trees,
And builds a road from earth to sky,
    Is prettier far than these.

Christina G. Rossetti

Illustration by Laura Logan

What Is Pink?

What is pink? A rose is pink
By the fountain's brink.
What is red? A poppy's red
In its barley bed.
What is blue? The sky is blue
Where the clouds float through.
What is white? A swan is white
Sailing in the light.
What is yellow? Pears are yellow,
Rich and ripe and mellow.
What is green? The grass is green,
With small flowers between.
What is violet? Clouds are violet
In the summer twilight.
What is orange? Why, an orange,
Just an orange!

Christina G. Rossetti

Illustration by Ashley Bryan

Open House

If I were a tree
I'd want to see
a bird with a song
on a branch of me.

I'd want a quick
little squirrel to run
up and down
and around, for fun.

I'd want the cub
of a bear to call,
and a porcupine, big,
and a tree toad, small.

I'd want a katydid
out of sight
on one of my leaves
to sing at night.

And down by my roots
I'd want a mouse
with six little mouselings
in her house.

Aileen L. Fisher

Illustration by Robert Quackenbush

The Little Rose Tree

Every rose on the little tree
Is making a different face at me!

Some look surprised when I pass by,
And others droop—but they are shy.

These two whose heads together press
Tell secrets I could never guess.

Some have their heads thrown back to sing,
And all the buds are listening.

I wonder if the gardener knows,
Or if he calls each just a rose?

Rachel Field

Illustration by Nancy Tafuri

Afternoon on a Hill

I will be the gladdest thing
    Under the sun!
I will touch a hundred flowers
    And not pick one.

I will look at cliffs and clouds
    With quiet eyes,
Watch the wind bow down the grass,
    And the grass rise.

And when lights begin to show
    Up from the town,
I will mark which must be mine,
    And then start down!

Edna St. Vincent Millay

Illustration by Dan Yaccarino

Metaphor

Morning is
a new sheet of paper
for you to write on.

Whatever you want to say,
all day,
until night
folds it up
and files it away.

The bright words and the dark words
are gone
until dawn
and a new day
to write on.

Eve Merriam

Illustration by David Gordon

Eyes in the Night

The moon came up on a summer's night
That was soft and dark except for the light
Of fireflies and the gleaming eyes
Of green-eyed cats and the amber eyes of wandering dogs
And the red eyes of frogs and the eye of the toad
Picked up by lights coming down the road,
Little emerald eyes, the gleaming eyes,
And the eyes of rabbits and foxes
And more and more flickering fireflies.
Then the car went by, and soon
There was only the light
Of a big warm moon
All over the summer night.

Margaret Wise Brown

Illustration by Dan Yaccarino

Sleeping Outdoors

Under the dark is a star,
Under the star is a tree,
Under the tree is a blanket,
And under the blanket is me.

Marchette Chute

Illustration by Aliki

The Star

Twinkle, twinkle, little star
How I wonder what you are!
Up above the world so high,
Like a diamond in the sky.

When the blazing sun is gone,
When he nothing shines upon,
Then you show your little light,
Twinkle, twinkle, all the night.

Then the traveller in the dark,
Thanks you for your tiny spark,
He could not see which way to go,
If you did not twinkle so.

In the dark blue sky you keep,
And often through my curtains peep,
For you never shut your eye,
Till the sun is in the sky.

As your bright and tiny spark,
Lights the traveller in the dark—
Though I know not what you are,
Twinkle, twinkle, little star.

Jane Taylor

Illustration by Laura Logan

Until We Built a Cabin

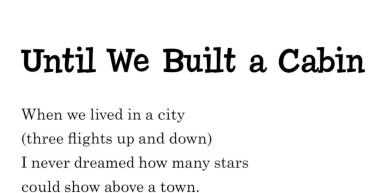

When we lived in a city
(three flights up and down)
I never dreamed how many stars
could show above a town.

When we moved to a village
where lighted streets were few,
I thought I could see ALL the stars,
but, oh, I never knew—

Until we built a cabin
where hills are high and far,
I never knew how many
        many
            stars there really are!

Aileen L. Fisher

Illustration by Chris Raschka

Wise

Whoever planned
the world was wise
to think of land
and seas and skies,

To plan a sun
and moon that could
be made to run
the way they should.

But how did He
have time for all
the things we see
that are so small . . .

Like flowers in parks
and flakes of snow
and little sparks
the fireflies show?

Aileen L. Fisher

Illustration by Derek Anderson

Taking Turns

When sun goes home
behind the trees,
and locks her shutters tight—

then stars come out
with silver keys
to open up the night.

Norma Farber

Illustration by Laura Logan

To Look at Any Thing

To look at any thing,
If you would know that thing,
You must look at it long:
To look at this green and say,
'I have seen spring in these
Woods,' will not do—you must
Be the thing you see:
You must be the dark snakes of
Stems and ferny plumes of leaves,
You must enter in
To the small silences between
The leaves,
You must take your time
And touch the very peace
They issue from.

John Moffitt

Hurt No Living Thing

Hurt no living thing:
Ladybird, nor butterfly,
Nor moth with dusty wing,
Nor cricket chirping cheerily,
Nor grasshopper so light of leap,
Nor dancing gnat, nor beetle fat,
Nor harmless worms that creep.

Christina G. Rossetti

Illustration by Aliki

Around
the Year

The Months

Thirty days hath September
April, June and November.
All the rest have thirty-one,
Excepting February alone,
Which has four and twenty-four
Till leap-year gives it one day more.

Anonymous

Illustration by Robert Quackenbush

New Year's Day

Last night, while we were fast asleep,
    The old year went away.
It can't come back again because
    A new one's come to stay.

Rachel Field

Illustration by Laura Logan

To My Valentine

If apples were pears,
And peaches were plums,
And the rose had a different name,
If tigers were bears,
And fingers were thumbs,
I'd love you just the same!

Anonymous

Illustration by Paul Meisel

March Winds and April Showers

March winds and April showers
Bring forth May flowers.

Mother Goose

Illustration by Robert Quackenbush

April Rain Song

Let the rain kiss you.
Let the rain beat upon
   your head with
   silver liquid drops.
Let the rain sing you a
   lullaby.

The rain makes still
   pools on the sidewalk.

The rain makes running
   pools in the gutter.
The rain plays a little
   sleep-song on our roof at
   night—

And I love the rain.

Langston Hughes

Illustration by Chris Raschka

Green Grass
& Dandelions

Never has the grass been so green
Bright and green and growing
Never have the dandelions been so yellow
Bright yellow
Constellations
Brave little lions
Suns in the grass
Dandelions
In the green green green green grass
Never has the grass been so green
Bright and green and growing.
In any spring.

Margaret Wise Brown

Illustration by Chris Raschka

Autumn

The morns are meeker than they were,
The nuts are getting brown;
The berry's cheek is plumper,
The rose is out of town.

The maple wears a gayer scarf,
The field a scarlet gown.
Lest I should be old-fashioned,
I'll put a trinket on.

Emily Dickinson

Illustration by Robert Quackenbush

October

O hushed October morning mild,
Thy leaves have ripened to the fall;
Tomorrow's wind, if it be wild,
Should waste them all.
The crows above the forest call;
Tomorrow they may form and go.
O hushed October morning mild,
Begin the hours of this day slow.
Make the day seem to us less brief.
Hearts not averse to being beguiled,
Beguile us in the way you know.
Release one leaf at break of day;
At noon release another leaf;
One from our trees, one far away.
Retard the sun with gentle mist;
Enchant the land with amethyst.
Slow, slow!
For the grapes' sake, if they were all,
Whose leaves already are burnt with frost,
Whose clustered fruit must else be lost—
For the grapes' sake along the wall.

Robert Frost

Illustration by Laura Logan

The Last Word of a Bluebird

As told to a child

As I went out a Crow
In a low voice said, "Oh,
I was looking for you.
How do you do?
I just came to tell you
To tell Lesley (will you?)
That her little Bluebird
Wanted me to bring word
That the north wind last night
That made the stars bright
And made ice on the trough
Almost made him cough
His tail feathers off.
He just had to fly!
But he sent her Good-by,
And said to be good,
And wear her red hood,
And look for skunk tracks
In the snow with an ax—
And do everything!
And perhaps in the spring
He would come back and sing."

Robert Frost

Illustration by Dan Yaccarino

I Heard a Bird Sing

I heard a bird sing
    In the dark of December
A magical thing
    And sweet to remember.

"We are nearer to Spring
    Than we were in September,"
I heard a bird sing
    In the dark of December.

Oliver Herford

Illustration by Nancy Tafuri

Thanksgiving Day

Over the river and through the wood,
   To grandfather's house we go;
         The horse knows the way
         To carry the sleigh
Through the white and drifted snow.

Over the river and through the wood—
   Oh, how the wind does blow!
         It stings the toes
         And bites the nose,
As over the ground we go.

L. Maria Child

Illustration by Nancy Tafuri

Stopping by Woods on a Snowy Evening

Whose woods these are I think I know.
His house is in the village though;
He will not see me stopping here
To watch his woods fill up with snow.

My little horse must think it queer
To stop without a farmhouse near
Between the woods and frozen lake
The darkest evening of the year.

He gives his harness bells a shake
To ask if there is some mistake.
The only other sound's the sweep
Of easy wind and downy flake.

The woods are lovely, dark and deep.
But I have promises to keep,
And miles to go before I sleep,
And miles to go before I sleep.

Robert Frost

Illustration by Derek Anderson

Happy Hanukkah!

Outside, snow is slowly, softly
Falling through the wintry night.
In the house, the brass menorah
Sparkles with the candlelight.
Children in a circle listen
To the wondrous stories told,
Of the daring Maccabeans
And the miracles of old.
In the kitchen, pancakes sizzle,
Turning brown, they'll soon be done.
Gifts are waiting to be opened,
Happy Hanukkah's begun.

Eva Grant

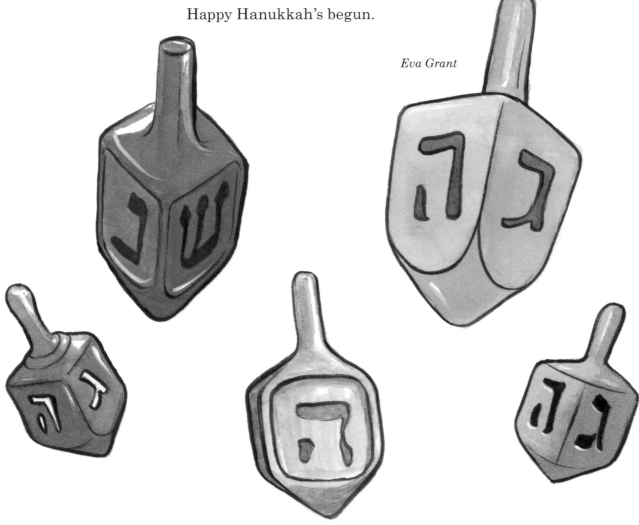

Illustration by Henry Cole

Christmas Song

O come little milk cows
O come to the barn
A baby is hungry
O do him no harm

O come little barn owls
O come to the barn
The wisest of babies
Is here keeping warm

O come all wild birds
Descend gentle dove
And all things from Heaven
To give him your love

O come little fishes
Flash out of the sea
A baby is smiling
On his mother's knee

O come little black sheep
O come right away
For all is forgiven
On this Christmas Day

Margaret Wise Brown

Illustration by Henry Cole

People and Places

City Song

I love the city with its cross patch of people,
I love the cathedral and its sky high steeple.

I love the carriages with horses prancing,
I love the toy stores with children dancing.

I love playing in the park,
I love skating until dark.

I love the colorful flags of many nations,
I love the painter and his beautiful creations.

I love the friendly policeman protecting us from crime.
I love the old clock tower that keeps our world in time.

I love the joggers and their fancy running shoes.
I love the baseball games and the fans that like to boo.

I love the sudden rains,
I love noisy trains.

I love the corner hot dog stand,
I love the street musician beating on his silver can.

I love the museums that share the world's treasures,
I love the concerts in the park that give us all such pleasure.

Sky scrapers,
Dream makers.

The city is my home.

Bill Martin Jr and Michael Sampson

Illustration by Paul Meisel

Skyscraper

Skyscraper, skyscraper,
Scrape me some sky:
Tickle the sun
While the stars go by.
Tickle the stars
While the sun's climbing high,
Then skyscraper, skyscraper
Scrape me some sky.

Dennis Lee

Illustration by Laura Logan

Subways Are People

Subways are people—

> People standing
> People sitting
> People swaying to and fro
> Some in suits
> Some in tatters
> People I will never know.

> Some with glasses
> Some without
> Boy with smile
> Girl with frown

> People dashing
> Steel flashing
> Up and down and 'round the
> town.

Subways are people—

> People old
> People new
> People always on the go
> Racing, running, rushing people
> People I will never know.

Lee Bennett Hopkins

Illustration by Dan Yaccarino

Climbing

The trunk of a tree
is the road for me
on a sunny summer day.

Up the bark
that is brown and dark
through tunnels of leaves that sway
and tickle my knees
in the trembly breeze,
that's where I make my way.

Leaves in my face
and twigs in my hair
in a squeeze of a place,
but I don't care!

Some people talk
of a summer walk
through clover and weeds and hay.

Some people stride
where the hills are wide
and the rocks are speckled gray.

But the trunk of a tree
is the road for me
on a sunny summer day.

Aileen L. Fisher

Illustration by Steven Kellogg

72

In the Woods

Silence of the deep green wood
Where little sounds are heard
The flutter of such tiny wings
The buzz and sudden springs
Of grasshoppers flying from the grass
Where the shining beetle traffics pass
Near the roots of the long green grass
And in the birch trees
The rustling gust of sunlit leaves
The silence of logs, the coldness of stones
Deep in the deep green wood alone
Where the little sounds are heard
And the terrible clap of the wings of a bird
Flying to break
The high silence
Of the still blue sky.

Margaret Wise Brown

Illustration by Nancy Tafuri

Knoxville, Tennessee

I always like summer
best
you can eat fresh corn
from daddy's garden
and okra
and greens
and cabbage
and lots of
barbecue
and buttermilk
and homemade ice-cream
at the church picnic

and listen to
gospel music
outside
at the church
homecoming
and you go to the mountains with
your grandmother
and go barefooted
and be warm
all the time
not only when you go to bed
and sleep

Nikki Giovanni

Illustration by Henry Cole

Child of the Sun

I am Child of sand and sun,
    of open space and sky,
Where mesa table-tops lie bare
    and purple buttes are high.
My blood flows back a thousand years
    to people strong and good
Who tamed this land of little rain
    where others never could.
We made our homes of rock and earth
    and worked the farms below,
Carried water from the stream
    that sometimes didn't flow.
We starved, we fought our enemies,
    but we loved and laughed and prayed,
And even in the darkest times,
    somehow . . . we stayed.
Then others came to change our lives,
    we struggled, kept our ways.
We loved our past, our ancient ones,
    and clung to yesterdays.
I am the child of my ancestors,
    proud child of sand and sun.
We make our home on mesa tops
    and my people . . . we are one!

Lillian M. Fisher

Illustration by Laura Logan

Postman's Song

What will the postman bring today?
A letter from a sailor who has sailed away
A letter with a stamp from Mandalay
And a funny postcard from Casco Bay
Oh, what will the postman bring next week?
A letter from a man who's afraid to speak
Or a package of fish from Chesapeake
Oh, what will the postman bring next week?
For
What he'll bring you'll never know
The mail may be fast or the mail may be slow
The wind may blow, and the snow may snow
But the mail must go through

Through snow and rain and sleet and hail
Seven little postmen carry the mail
Through sleet and snow and dark of night
Put a stamp on your letter and seal it tight

Margaret Wise Brown

Illustration by Robert Quackenbush

The Park

I'm glad that I
    Live near a park

For in the winter
    After dark

The park lights shine
    As bright and still

As dandelions
    On a hill.

James S. Tippett

Illustration by Paul Meisel

So Many Nights

So many nights.
Blue nights,
Brown nights,
And the sudden lights
In deep black nights
Of stars
And cars
And airplanes
And soft gray nights when it rains
And blue nights with a foggy moon
Smoking in the trees

And pink and red nights
Above great cities
And silver nights all filled with stars
And misty nights when a white mist
Drifts
And lifts over the white-topped fields
And purple nights beyond the lights
Of your own room
And blue snowy nights
And night that is just
Dark bright night.

Margaret Wise Brown

Illustration by Laura Logan

Manhattan Lullaby

Now lighted windows climb the dark,
    The streets are dim with snow,
Like tireless beetles, amber-eyed
    The creeping taxis go.
Cars roar through caverns made of steel,
    Shrill sounds the siren horn,
And people dance and die and wed—
    And boys like you are born.

Rachel Field

Illustration by Chris Raschka

79

Once Upon a Time

The Storyteller came to town
To share his gifts sublime,
    Tell it again, Storyteller,
    Tell it again,
Onceupona
Onceupona
Onceuponatime,
    Tell it again, Storyteller
    Tell it again,
Doors flew open to him,
Kings begged him not depart,
And children tucked his stories
In the pockets of their heart,
Tell it again, Storyteller
    Tell it again,
Onceupona
Onceupona
Onceuponatime,
Tell it again, Storyteller
    Tell it again,
He told of scary ghosts
And of witches who became toast,
Of knights of old
And outlaws bold.
Oh
Onceupona
Onceupona
Onceuponatime,
    Tell it again, Storyteller,
    Tell it again.

Bill Martin Jr and Michael Sampson

Illustration by David Gordon

School Time

First Day of School

I wonder
if my drawing
will be as good as theirs.

I wonder
if they'll like me
or just be full of stares.

I wonder
if my teacher
will look like Mom or Gram.

I wonder
if my puppy
will wonder
where I am.

Aileen L. Fisher

Illustration by Aliki

Pick Me, Please

Teacher
Teacher
Pick me please
I know the name
Is Hercules

Ask me
Ask me
Just this once
I'll prove to you
I'm not a dunce

My hand
My hand
Is waving high
Won't you catch it
With your eye

My heart
My heart
Is beating fast
Just waiting
For you to ask . . .

Me?
You picked me?
Wow!
Me!

Kalli Dakos

Illustration by Aliki

SOS

Sammy's head is pounding—
Sammy's in pain—
A long division's got
Stuck in his brain—
Call for the locksmith
Call the engineer
Call for the plumber
To suck out his ear,
Call the brain surgeon
To pry out the mess,
Call out the Coast Guard
SOS,
Because—
Sammy's head is pounding—
Sammy's in pain—
A long division's got
Stuck in his brain.

Beverly McLoughland

Illustration by Laura Logan

Take a Number

from

Imagine a world
Without mathematics:
No rulers or scales,
No inches or feet,
No dates or numbers
On house or street,
No prices or weights,
No determining heights,
No hours running through
Days and nights.
No zero, no birthdays,
No way to subtract
All of the guesswork
Surrounding the fact.
No sizes for shoes,
Or suit or hat. . . .
Wouldn't it be awful
To live like that?

Mary O'Neill

Illustration by Derek Anderson

I Brought a Worm

Jane brought a baseball bat
And a ball for sharing time.

But I brought a worm!

Rich brought a goldfish bowl
Without a goldfish.

But I brought a worm!

Lizzy brought an egg with a yolk
And an egg without a yolk.

But I brought a worm!

Joe brought an eraser shaped like a knife
And an olive sandwich.

But I brought a worm!

Jane showed us how to hit
The ball with the bat.

Rich put the class turtle
In the goldfish bowl.

Lizzy showed us how to pick an egg
And take the yolk out.

Joe tried to cut his sandwich
With his eraser knife.

But I ate the worm!
Right there in front of everyone
I ate the worm!

(It was a candy worm.)

Kalli Dakos

Illustration by Paul Meisel

Ten Little Caterpillars

The first little caterpillar
crawled into a bower.

The second little caterpillar
wriggled up a flower.

The third little caterpillar
climbed a cabbage head.

Illustration by Lois Ehlert

The fourth little caterpillar
found a melon bed.

The fifth little caterpillar
sailed a garden pool.

The sixth little caterpillar
was carried off to school.

The seventh little caterpillar
met a hungry wren.

The eighth little caterpillar
was frightened by a hen.

Illustration by Lois Ehlert

The ninth little caterpillar
fell into the sea.

The tenth little caterpillar
scaled an apple tree,
and hung there patiently,
until by and by,
the tenth little caterpillar
became a butterfly.

Bill Martin Jr

Illustration by Lois Ehlert

Word Builder

Begin your new construction
with twenty-six letters.
Hammer *a* through *z* into words.
Pile your words like blocks
into sentence towers—
measure some tall,
saw others short.
Mortar each sentence
with punctuation,
then frame your sentences
into paragraph villages,
stack your paragraphs
into chapter cities.
Keep on building
words into sentences
sentences into paragraphs,
paragraphs into chapters
until you have created
a whole world of book.

Ann Whitford Paul

Illustration by Laura Logan

Under the Microscope

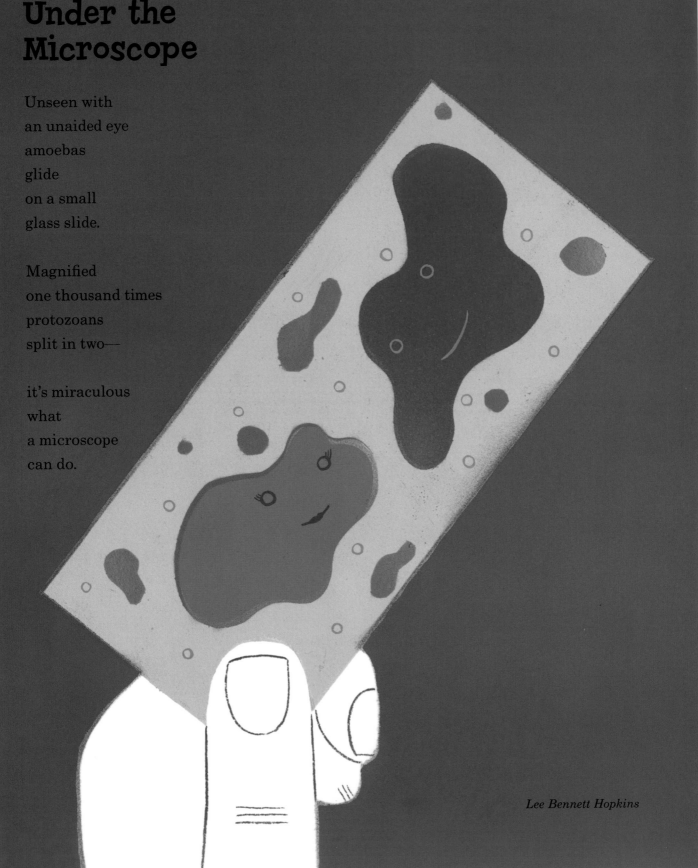

Unseen with
an unaided eye
amoebas
glide
on a small
glass slide.

Magnified
one thousand times
protozoans
split in two—

it's miraculous
what
a microscope
can do.

Lee Bennett Hopkins

Illustration by Dan Yaccarino

Poor Substitute

Gretchen had taken Freddy's chair,
Andrew's desk has no one there.

Sally was fighting for Tommy's space,
She won the battle and took his place.

Daryl is working at Jennie's desk,
And Joe just finished Maria's test.

Substitute teacher, you'd better beware,
Alicia just plopped in the teacher's chair.

Kalli Dakos

Illustration by Aliki

Me and My Feelings

The Swing

How do you like to go up in a swing,
    Up in the air so blue?
Oh, I do think it is the pleasantest thing
    Ever a child can do!

Up in the air and over the wall,
    Till I can see so wide,
Rivers and trees and cattle and all
    Over the countryside—

Till I look down on the garden green,
Down on the roof so brown—
Up in the air I go flying again,
Up in the air and down!

Robert Louis Stevenson

Illustration by Steven Kellogg

I've Got an Itch

I've got an itch, a wretched itch,
no other itch could match it,
it itches in the one spot which
I cannot reach, to scratch it.

Jack Prelutsky

Illustration by Henry Cole

Papa Says

Papa
Says rain
Makes things grow.

I stood out in the rain
All morning
With my toes in the mud,
But Grandma says I really
Didn't get any Bigger.
It's just that my pants
Shrunk.

Libby Stopple

Illustration by Aliki

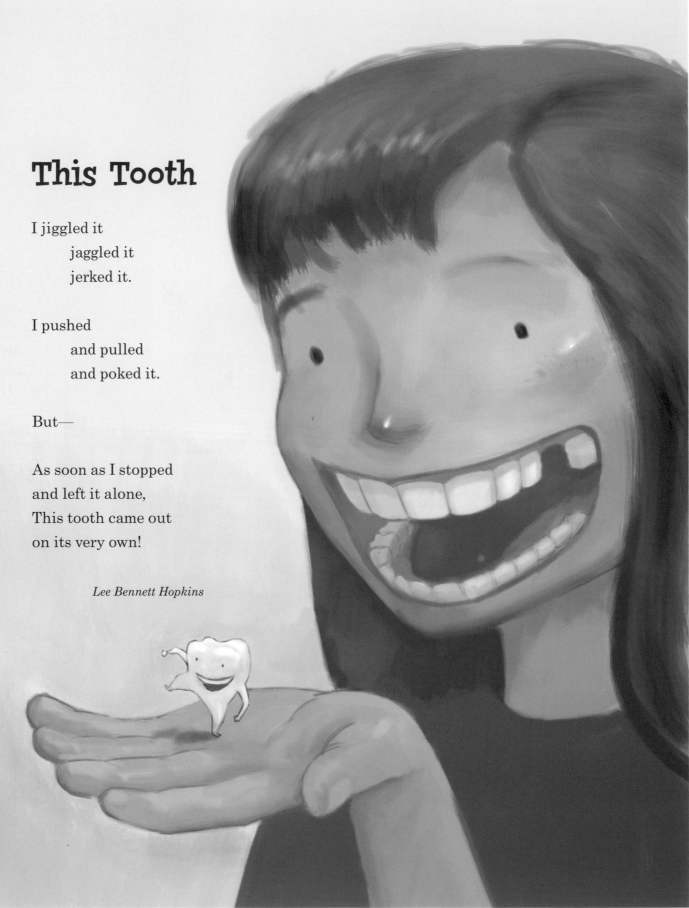

This Tooth

I jiggled it
    jaggled it
    jerked it.

I pushed
    and pulled
    and poked it.

But—

As soon as I stopped
and left it alone,
This tooth came out
on its very own!

Lee Bennett Hopkins

Illustration by David Gordon

Bursting

We've laughed until my cheeks are tight.
We've laughed until my stomach's sore.
If we could only stop we might
Remember what we're laughing for.

Dorothy Aldis

Illustration by Paul Meisel

My Shadow

I have a little shadow that goes in and out with me,
And what can be the use of him is more than I can see.
He is very, very like me from the heels up to the head;
And I see him jump before me, when I jump into my bed.

The funniest thing about him is the way he likes to grow—
Not at all like proper children, which is always very slow;
For he sometimes shoots up taller like an India-rubber ball,
And he sometimes gets so little that there's none of him at all.

He hasn't got a notion of how children ought to play,
And can only make a fool of me in every sort of way.
He stays so close beside me, he's a coward you can see;
I'd think shame to stick to nursie as that shadow sticks to me!

One morning, very early, before the sun was up,
I rose and found the shining dew on every buttercup;
But my lazy little shadow, like an arrant sleepyhead,
Had stayed at home behind me and was fast asleep in bed.

Robert Louis Stevenson

Illustration by Aliki

I Am Running in a Circle

I am running in a circle
and my feet are getting sore,
and my head is
spinning
spinning
as it's never spun before,
I am
dizzy
dizzy
dizzy.
Oh! I cannot bear much more,
I am trapped in a
revolving
. . . volving
. . . volving
. . . volving door!

Jack Prelutsky

Illustration by David Gordon

Tiptoe

Yesterday I skipped all day,
The day before I ran,
Today I'm going to tiptoe
Everywhere I can.
I'll tiptoe down the stairway.
I'll tiptoe through the door.
I'll tiptoe to the living room
And give an awful roar
And my father, who is reading,
Will jump up from his chair
And mumble something silly like
"I didn't see you there."
I'll tiptoe to my mother
And give a little cough
And when she spins to see me
Why, I'll softly tiptoe off.
I'll tiptoe through the meadows,
Over hills and yellow sands
And when my toes get tired
Then I'll tiptoe on my hands.

Karla Kuskin

Illustration by Chris Raschka

My Dog

His nose is short and scrubby;
    His ears hang rather low,
And he always brings the stick back,
    No matter how far you throw.

He gets spanked rather often
    For things he shouldn't do,
Like lying-on-beds, and barking,
    And eating up shoes when they're new.

He always wants to be going
    Where he isn't supposed to go.
He tracks up the house when it's snowing—
    Oh, puppy, I love you so.

Marchette Chute

Illustration by Aliki

Vacation

In my head I hear a humming:
Summer, summer, summer's coming.
Soon we're going on vacation
But there is a complication:
Day by day the problem's growing—
We don't know yet where we're going!

Mother likes the country best;
That's so she can read and rest.
Dad thinks resting is a bore;
He's for fishing at the shore.
Sailing is my brother's pick;
Sailing makes my sister sick;
She says swimming's much more cool,
Swimming in a swimming pool.
As for me, why, I don't care,
I'd be happy anywhere!

In my head I hear a humming:
Summer, summer, summer's coming.
Soon we're going on vacation
But we have a complication:
Day by day the problem's growing—
Where oh where will we be going?

Mary Ann Hoberman

Illustration by Derek Anderson

Kick a Little Stone

When you are walking by yourself
Here's something nice to do:
Kick a little stone and watch it
Hop ahead of you.

The little stone is round and white,
Its shadow round and blue,
Along the sidewalk over the cracks
The shadow bounces too.

Dorothy Aldis

Illustration by Steven Kellogg

I Keep Three Wishes Ready

I keep three wishes ready,
Lest I should chance to meet,
Any day a fairy
Coming down the street.

I'd hate to have a stammer,
Or have to think them out,
For it's very hard to think things up
When a fairy is about.

And I'd hate to lose my wishes,
For fairies fly away,
And perhaps I'd never have a chance
On any other day.

So I keep three wishes ready,
Lest I should chance to meet,
Any day a fairy
Coming down the street.

Annette Wynne

Illustration by Laura Logan

The Dark

It's always
dark
around my bed
and darkest
where I put my head;
and there are nights
when strange sounds
call
inside
the hollow
of the wall
and creaking noises
from inside
the closet
where
the
nightmares
hide;
so after I have said
my prayers
and hear them
talking from
downstairs,
I look around
so I can see
where everything
I know
should be—
especially
along the floor,
the crack of light
beneath the door.

Myra Cohn Livingston

Illustration by Chris Raschka

Bed in Summer

In winter I get up at night
And dress by yellow candle-light.
In summer quite the other way,
I have to go to bed by day.

I have to go to bed and see
The birds still hopping on the tree,
Or hear the grown-up people's feet
Still going past me in the street.

And does it not seem hard to you,
When all the sky is clear and blue,
And I should like so much to play,
To have to go to bed by day?

Robert Louis Stevenson

Illustration by Henry Cole

If I Were in Charge of the World

If I were in charge of the world
I'd cancel oatmeal,
Monday mornings,
Allergy shots, and also
Sara Steinberg.

If I were in charge of the world
There'd be brighter night lights,
Healthier hamsters, and
Basketball baskets forty eight inches lower.

If I were in charge of the world
You wouldn't have lonely.
You wouldn't have clean.
You wouldn't have bedtimes.
Or "Don't punch your sister."
You wouldn't even have sisters.

If I were in charge of the world
A chocolate sundae with whipped cream and nuts
   would be a vegetable
All 007 movies would be G.
And a person who sometimes forgot to brush,
And sometimes forgot to flush,
Would still be allowed to be
In charge of the world.

Judith Viorst

Illustration by Laura Logan

Painting the Gate

I painted the mailbox. That was fun.
I painted it postal blue.
Then I painted the gate.
I painted a spider that got on the gate.
I painted his mate.
I painted the ivy around the gate.
Some stones I painted blue,
and part of the cat as he rubbed by.
I painted my hair. I painted my shoe.
I painted the slats, both front and back,
all their beveled edges, too.
I painted the numbers on the gate—
I shouldn't have, but it was too late.
I painted the posts, each side and top,
I painted the hinges, the handle, the lock,
several ants and a moth asleep in a crack.
At last I was through.
I'd painted the gate
shut, me out, with both hands dark blue,
as well as my nose, which,
early on, because of a sudden itch,
got painted. But wait!
I had painted the gate.

May Swenson

Illustration by David Gordon

My Star

My star comes out
When I'm in bed,
> There is a place to put my head
> where I can watch it twinkle
> high
> in one small windowpane of sky.

Myra Cohn Livingston

Illustration by Paul Meisel

Dreamer

I take my dreams
And make of them a bronze vase,
And a wide round fountain
With a beautiful statue in its center,
And a song with a broken heart,
And I ask you:
Do you understand my dreams?
Sometimes you say you do
And sometimes you say you don't.
Either way
It doesn't matter.
I continue to dream.

Langston Hughes

Illustration by David Gordon

Family and Home

Grandpa's Stories

The pictures on the television
Do not make me dream as well
As the stories without pictures
Grandpa knows how to tell.

Even if he does not know
What makes a Spaceman go,
Grandpa says back in his time
Hamburgers only cost a dime,
Ice cream cones a nickel,
And a penny for a pickle.

Langston Hughes

Illustration by Ashley Bryan

in daddy's arms

in daddy's arms i am tall
& close to the sun & warm
in daddy's arms

in daddy's arms
i can see over the fence out back
i can touch the bottom leaves of the big magnolia tree
in Cousin Sukie's yard
in daddy's arms

in my daddy's arms the moon is close
closer at night time when I can almost touch it
when it grins back at me from the wide twinkling
skies

in daddy's arms i am tall
taller than Benny & my friends Ade & George
taller than Uncle Billy
& best of all
i am eye-ball-even-steven with my big brother Jamal

in my daddy's arms
i am strong & dark like him & laughing
happier than the circus clowns
with red painted grins
when daddy spins me round & round
& the whole world is crazy upside down
i am big and strong & proud like him
in daddy's arms
my daddy

Folami Abiade

Illustration by Dan Yaccarino

Promises

Dear Daddy,
I'm sorry I did not do what you told me to do.
If I do better
Can I still be your little boy?

Dear Son,
You will be
My little boy
For all of your little-boy days.
And when
You are no longer a little boy
I will still be your daddy.

David A. Anderson

Illustration by David Gordon

A Social Mixer

Father said, "Heh, heh! I'll fix her!"—
Threw Mother in the concrete mixer.

She whirled about and called, "Come hither!"
It looked like fun. He jumped in with her.

Then in to join that dizzy dance
Jumped Auntie Bea and Uncle Anse.

In leaped my little sister Lena
And Chuckling Chuck, her pet hyena.

Even Granmaw Fanshaw felt a yearning
To do some high-speed overturning.

All shouted through the motor's whine,
"Aw come on in—the concrete's fine!"

I jumped in too and got all scrambly.
What a crazy mixed-up family!

X. J. Kennedy

Illustration by Henry Cole

My Little Sister

My little sister
Likes to eat.
But when she does
She's not too neat.
The trouble is
She doesn't know
Exactly where
The food should go!

William Wise

Illustration by Aliki

Some Things Don't Make Any Sense at All

My mom says I'm her sugarplum.

My mom says I'm her lamb.

My mom says I'm completely perfect

Just the way I am.

My mom says I'm a super-special wonderful terrific

little guy.

My mom just had another baby.

Why?

Judith Viorst

Illustration by Laura Logan

I Love You Little

I love you little,
I love you lots,
My love for you would fill ten pots,
Fifteen buckets,
Sixteen cans,
Three teacups
And four dishpans.

Anonymous

Illustration by Robert Quackenbush

Food for Me

On Eating Porridge Made of Peas

Peas porridge hot,
Peas porridge—hold!
Who eats peas porridge?
Who is so bold?

I know I never munch
Peas porridge for my lunch,
&, as for dinner,
Peas porridge is no winner.

Peas porridge ice cold,
Peas porridge tepid,
Who eats peas porridge?
Who could be so stupid?

Peas porridge nine days old—ugh!
I think I'd prefer to eat a rug.

Louis Phillips

Illustration by Paul Meisel

I Eat My Peas with Honey

I eat my peas with honey,
I've done it all my life.
It makes the peas taste funny,
But it keeps them on my knife.

Anonymous

Illustration by Steven Kellogg

Speak Clearly

You're old enough to know, my son,
    It's really awfully rude
If someone speaks when both his cheeks
    Are jammed and crammed with food.

Your mother asked you how you liked
    The onions in the stew.
You stuffed your mouth with raisin bread
    And mumbled, "Vewee goo."

Then when she asked you what you said,
    You took a drink of milk,
And all that we could understand
    Was, "Uggle gluggle skwilk."

And now you're asking me if you
    Can have more lemon jello.
Please listen carefully. "Yes, ifoo
    Arstilla ungwy fello."

Martin Gardner

Illustration by Aliki

Let There Be Pizza on Earth

Let there be pizza on earth,
and let it be eaten by me,
Let there be pizza on earth,
as far as the eye can see,
With ham and pepperoni,
mozzarella cheese,
Add some mushrooms and olives,
But hold the anchovies please!

Let pizza be eaten by me,
Let this be the moment now,
With every bite I take,
Let this be my solemn vow:
To take each pizza,
and eat each pizza,
in perfect ecstasy,
Oh, let there be pizza on earth,
And let it be eaten by me!

David Canzoneri and Bill Martin Jr

Illustration by Laura Logan

Mummy Slept Late and Daddy Fixed Breakfast

Daddy fixed the breakfast.
He made us each a waffle.
It looked like gravel pudding.
It tasted something awful.

"Ha, ha," he said, "I'll try again.
This time I'll get it right."
But what *I* got was in between
Bituminous and anthracite.

"A little too well done? Oh well,
I'll have to start all over."
That time what landed on my plate
Looked like a manhole cover.

I tried to cut it with a fork:
The fork gave off a spark.
I tried a knife and twisted it
Into a question mark.

I tried it with a hack-saw.
I tried it with a torch.
It didn't even make a dent.
It didn't even scorch.

The next time Dad gets breakfast
When Mommy's sleeping late,
I think I'll skip the waffles.
I'd sooner eat the plate!

John Ciardi

Illustration by Laura Logan

Oodles of Noodles

I love noodles. Give me oodles.
Make a mound up to the sun.
Noodles are my favorite foodles.
I eat noodles by the ton.

Lucia and James L. Hymes Jr.

Illustration by Chris Raschka

Herbert Glerbett

Herbert Glerbett, rather round,
swallowed sherbet by the pound,
fifty pounds of lemon sherbet
went inside of Herbert Glerbett.

With that glob inside his lap
Herbert Glerbett took a nap,
and as he slept, the boy dissolved,
and from the mess a thing evolved—

a thing that is a ghastly green,
a thing the world had never seen,
a puddle thing, a gooey pile
of something strange that does not smile.

Now if you're wise, and if you're sly,
you'll swiftly pass this creature by,
it is no longer Herbert Glerbett.
Whatever it is, do not disturb it.

Jack Prelutsky

Illustration by Dan Yaccarino

O Sliver
of Liver

O sliver of liver,
Get lost! Go away!
You tremble and quiver
O sliver of liver—
You set me a-shiver
And spoil my day—
O sliver of liver,
Get lost! Go away!

Myra Cohn Livingston

Illustration by Henry Cole

139

Beans,
Beans,
Beans

Baked beans,
Butter beans,
Big fat lima beans,
Long thin string beans.
Those are just a few.
Green beans,
Black beans,
Big fat kidney beans,
Red hot chili beans,
Jumping beans too.
Pea beans,
Pinto beans,
Don't forget shelly beans.
Last of all, best of all,
I like jelly beans!

Lucia and James L. Hymes Jr.

Illustration by Derek Anderson

Nonsense

Norman Norton's Nostrils

Oh, Norman Norton's nostrils
Are powerful and strong;
Hold on to your belongings
If he should come along.

And do not ever let him
Inhale with all his might,
Or else your pens and pencils
Will disappear from sight.

Right up his nose they'll vanish;
Your future will be black.
Unless he gets the sneezes,
You'll *never* get them back!

Colin West

Illustration by Chris Raschka

Kitty Caught a Caterpillar

Kitty caught a caterpillar,
Kitty caught a snail,
Kitty caught a turtle,
by its tiny turtle tail,
Kitty caught a cricket
with a sticky bit of thread,
she tried to catch a bumblebee,
the bee caught her instead.

Jack Prelutsky

Illustration by Paul Meisel

Snail's Pace

Maybe it's so
that snails are slow:
they trudge along and tarry.

But isn't it true
you'd slow up, too,
if you had a house to carry?

Aileen L. Fisher

Illustration by Steven Kellogg

Dickery Dean

"What's the matter
    With Dickery Dean?
He jumped right into
    The washing machine!"

"Nothing's the matter
    With Dickery Dean—
He dove in dirty,
    And he jumped out clean!"

Dennis Lee

Illustration by Robert Quackenbush

Crooked Man

There was a crooked man,
    And he walked a crooked mile,
He found a crooked sixpence
    Against a crooked stile;
He bought a crooked cat,
    Which caught a crooked mouse,
And they all lived together
    In a little crooked house.

Mother Goose

Illustration by Robert Quackenbush

A Mouse in Her Room

A mouse in her room woke Miss Dowd.
She was frightened and screamed very loud.
Then a happy thought hit her—
To scare off the critter
She sat up in bed and meowed.

Anonymous

Illustration by Derek Anderson

Tombstone

Here lies
A bully
Who wasn't so wise.

He picked on
A fellow
Who was his own size.

Lucia and James L. Hymes Jr.

Illustration by Paul Meisel

Eat-It-All Elaine

I went away last August
To summer camp in Maine,
And there I met a camper
Called Eat-it-all Elaine.
Although Elaine was quiet,
She liked to cause a stir
By acting out the nickname
Her camp-mates gave to her.

The day of our arrival
At Cabin Number Three
When girls kept coming over
To greet Elaine and me,
She took a piece of Kleenex
And calmly chewed it up,
Then strolled outside the cabin
And ate a buttercup.

Elaine, from that day forward,
Was always in command.
On hikes, she'd eat some birch-bark
On swims, she'd eat some sand.

At meals, she'd swallow prune-pits
And never have a pain,
While everyone around her
Would giggle, "Oh, Elaine!"

One morning, berry-picking,
A bug was in her pail,
And though we thought for certain
Her appetite would fail,
Elaine said, "Hmm, a stinkbug."
And while we murmured, "Ooh,"
She ate her pail of berries
And ate the stinkbug, too.

The night of Final Banquet
When counselors were handing
Awards to different children
Whom they believed outstanding,
To every *thinking* person
At summer camp in Maine
The Most Outstanding Camper
Was Eat-it-all Elaine.

Kaye Starbird

Illustration by Henry Cole

The Folk Who Live in Backward Town

The folk who live in Backward Town
Are inside out and upside down.
They wear their hats inside their heads
And go to sleep beneath their beds.
They only eat the apple peeling
And take their walks across the ceiling.

Mary Ann Hoberman

154

The Folk Who Live in Backward Town

The folk who live in Backward Town
Are inside out and upside down.
They wear their hats inside their heads
And go to sleep beneath their beds.
They only eat the apple peeling
And take their walks across the ceiling.

Mary Ann Hoberman

Illustration by Steven Kellogg

155

Mother Goose

Old Mother Hubbard

Old Mother Hubbard
Went to the cupboard,
To fetch her poor dog a bone;
But when she got there
The cupboard was bare
And so the poor dog had none.

She went to the baker's
    To buy him some bread;
But when she came back
    He stood on his head.

She went to the hatter's
    To buy him a hat;
But when she came back
    He was feeding the cat.

She went to the fruiter's
    To buy him fruit;
But when she came back
    He was playing the flute.

She went to the barber's
    To buy him a wig;
But when she came back
    He was dancing a jig.

She went to the tailor's
    To buy him a coat;
But when she came back
    He was riding a goat.

The dame made a curtsey,
    The dog made a bow;
The dame said, Your Servant,
    The dog said, Bow-bow.

Adapted by Bill Martin Jr and Michael Sampson

Illustration by Robert Quackenbush

Knock on the Door

Knock on the door,
Peek in.
Lift the latch,
Time to begin!

Mother Goose

Wee Willie Winkie

Wee Willie Winkie runs through the town,
Upstairs and downstairs in his nightgown,
Rapping at the window, crying through the lock,
Are the children all in bed, for now it's eight o'clock?

Mother Goose

Illustration by Laura Logan

Hey Diddle, Diddle

Hey diddle, diddle,
The cat and the fiddle,
The cow jumped over the moon;
The little dog laughed
To see such sport,
And the dish ran away with the spoon.

Mother Goose

Illustration by Steven Kellogg

Jack Be Nimble

Jack be nimble,
　Jack be quick,
Jack jump over
　The candlestick.

Mother Goose

Illustration by Paul Meisel

King Cole

Old King Cole
Was a merry old soul,
And a merry old soul was he;
He called for his pipe,
And he called for his bowl,
And he called for his fiddlers three.

Every fiddler he had a fiddle,
And a very fine fiddle had he;
Oh, there's none so rare
As can compare
With King Cole and his fiddlers three.

Mother Goose

Illustration by David Gordon

Star Light

Star light, star bright,
First star I see tonight,
I wish I may, I wish I might,
Have the wish I wish tonight.

Mother Goose

Illustration by Ashley Bryan

Little Bo-Peep

Little Bo-Peep has lost her sheep,
And doesn't know where to find them;
Leave them alone, and they'll come home,
Bringing their tails behind them.

Little Bo-Peep fell fast asleep,
And dreamt she heard them bleating;
But when she awoke, she found it a joke,
For they were still a-fleeting.

Mother Goose

Illustration by Derek Anderson

Little Boy Blue

Little Boy Blue,
Come blow your horn.
The sheep's in the meadow,
The cow's in the corn.
Where is the boy
Who looks after the sheep?
He's under a haystack,
Fast asleep.
Will you wake him?
No, not I,
For if I do,
He's sure to cry.

Mother Goose

Black Sheep

Baa, baa, black sheep,
Have you any wool?
Yes sir, yes, sir,
Three bags full;
One for the master,
And one for the dame,
And one for the little boy
Who lives down the lane.

Mother Goose

Illustration by Derek Anderson

Song of Sixpence

Sing a song of sixpence,
A pocket full of rye;
Four and twenty blackbirds
Baked in a pie!

When the pie was opened
The birds began to sing;
Now wasn't that a dainty dish
To set before the king?

The king was in his counting-house
Counting out his money;
The queen was in the parlour,
Eating bread and honey.

The maid was in the garden,
Hanging out the clothes;
When down came a blackbird
And snipped off her nose.

Mother Goose

My Brother Was a Fisherman

My brother was a fisherman,
he fished in the sea,
and all the fish that he could catch,
were one, two, three.

My brother brought the fishes home,
he brought them from the shore,
When seven sat to savor them,
he wished he had caught some more!

Mother Goose

Illustration by Henry Cole

Hickory, Dickory, Dock

Hickory, dickory, dock,
The mouse ran up the clock.
    The clock struck one,
    The mouse ran down,
Hickory, dickory, dock.

Mother Goose

Illustration by Chris Raschka

The Tuft of Flowers

I went to turn the grass once after one
Who mowed it in the dew before the sun.

The dew was gone that made his blade so keen
Before I came to view the leveled scene.

I looked for him behind an isle of trees;
I listened for his whetstone on the breeze.

But he had gone his way, the grass all mown,
And I must be, as he had been—alone,

'As all must be,' I said within my heart,
'Whether they work together or apart.'

But as I said it, swift there passed me by
On noiseless wing a bewildered butterfly,

Seeking with memories grown dim o'er night
Some resting flower of yesterday's delight.

And once I marked his flight go round and round,
As where some flower lay withering on the ground.

And then he flew as far as eye could see,
And then on tremulous wing came back to me.

I thought of questions that have no reply,
And would have turned to toss the grass to dry;

But he turned first, and led my eye to look
At a tall tuft of flowers beside a brook,

A leaping tongue of bloom the scythe had spared
Beside a reedy brook the scythe had bared.

The mower in the dew had loved them thus,
By leaving them to flourish, not for us,

Nor yet to draw one thought of ours to him.
But from sheer morning gladness at the brim.

The butterfly and I had lit upon,
Nevertheless, a message from the dawn,

That made me hear the wakening birds around,
And hear his long scythe whispering to the ground,

And feel a spirit kindred to my own;
So that henceforth I worked no more alone;

But glad with him, I worked as with his aid,
And weary, sought at noon with him the shade;

And dreaming, as it were, held brotherly speech
With one whose thought I had not hoped to reach.

'Men work together,' I told him from the heart,
'Whether they work together or apart.'

Robert Frost

Illustration by Steven Kellogg

Afterword

When I think of Bill Martin Jr, I think of an endearing and immensely generous spirit. He was an ardent champion of teachers, and he was dedicated to empowering them to join him in his mission to introduce and continually expose children to the beauty, emotional richness, and compelling music of language.

Bill, the person, was in perfect harmony with his dedication to his work and with the unpretentious joy he derived from sharing his own creativity and encouraging those around him to rejoice in theirs. That dedication was palpable when one was in his presence! But it was the playfulness, merriment, and sparkle that he so often brought to his observations and conversations that made the ideas he espoused *irresistible*! One of his greatest contributions was to make his conviction about the importance of quality literature for all children so compelling that anyone who heard him speak was inspired to dedicate themselves with renewed fervor to making a difference in the lives of children.

After being exposed to Bill, authors and artists resolved to raise the standards they set for themselves, and to create books that would aspire to a higher level of eloquence, excellence, and beauty. After hearing Bill speak, teachers, librarians, and educators saw their mission with a new clarity. They rededicated themselves to encouraging, illuminating, and inspiring the children in their classrooms with a special emphasis on helping them to become enthusiastic about the development of their reading, writing, and communicative skills.

Bill understood that education is in many ways an art form and that teaching is theater. He understood that educators, authors, and artists are members of a creative team dedicated to helping children discover their unique expressive abilities by recognizing, owning, and celebrating the power of language and the magic of story.

—Steven Kellogg

INDEX OF TITLES

INDEX OF FIRST LINES

INDEX OF AUTHORS